7. A Time for a Change

Ryan suddenly smashed his football high up into the air against the ceiling, cracking one of the light fittings.

"Hey, you kids!" he yelled at the top of his voice. "Wake up! It's time for a change round here. You ain't never seen nothing like this..."

Ryan was quite right. The students had been taught about the rules of football, as far as their teachers understood the game from surviving records. There was even a set of small, netted goals at each end of the hall. But what they soon saw happening in front of their own goggling eyes took them by complete surprise. It stunned the watching teachers, too.

Join the Time Rangers on tour!

In the Peak District:

1. A Shot in the Dark
2. A Blast from the Past
3. A Race Against Time
4. A Ghost of a Chance

In the Cotswolds:

5. A Toss of the Coin
6. A Sting in the Tale

In London:

8. A Fate Worse Than Death

TIME RANGERS

7. A Time for a Change

Rob Childs

DAZZA
GOALKEEPER — 1

WORM
RIGHT-BACK — 2

STOPPER
CENTRE-BACK — 5

RAKESH
RIGHT-MIDFIELD — 4

MR STOPPARD
MANAGER

JACKO
CENTRE-MIDFIELD — 8

SPEEDIE
RIGHT-WINGER — 7

RYAN
CENTRE-FORWARD — 9

ANIL
LEFT-WINGER — 11

MR THOMAS
MANAGER

For my wife Joy, with special thanks

Scholastic Children's Books,
Commonwealth House,
1–19 New Oxford Street,
London WC1A 1NU, UK
A division of Scholastic Ltd
London ~ New York ~ Toronto ~ Sydney ~ Auckland

First published in the UK by Scholastic Ltd, 1998

ISBN 0 590 11126 4

Typeset by DP Photosetting, Aylesbury, Bucks.
Printed by Cox & Wyman Ltd, Reading, Berks.

10 9 8 7 6 5 4 3 2 1

1 Time

"Good stop!" cried Jacko. "Time. Don't panic."

The captain signalled to his keeper that the ball was dead. Nobody else was allowed to enter the semicircular goal area.

Dazza breathed a sigh of relief. He was quite pleased with his save, but normally he'd have been punished for letting the ball squirm out of his grasp. He picked it up and looked around for a blue shirt in space.

"C'mon, get moving!" he yelled to spur his Rangers teammates into action.

Jacko made a decoy run to the left and Ryan broke clear up front, but Dazza whisked the ball away underarm out to his right instead.

"Take it, Worm. Go, go, go!"

Worm obeyed. He took the ball in his stride and nipped past an opponent by playing a quick one-two off the boards along the side of the pitch. Then he went and spoiled his good work with a lofted centre.

The referee's whistle sounded instantly. "Over head height," he ruled. "Free-kick to Reds."

"Steady, Worm," Jacko called out. "Twice you've done that now."

The defender was finding it difficult to break the habit of aiming high crosses towards Ryan's head. Their leading scorer in the Under-13 Sunday League loved the ball in the air.

"Think!" came the bellow from behind the boards. "Keep it down."

Mr Thomas, Ryan's dad and joint manager of Tanfield Rangers, was red in the face from frustration. He could barely believe they were losing 1–0 after creating so many chances. What made it worse was that his own son had missed most of them.

The half-time break was timely. It enabled them to regroup and gave Mr Stoppard, the co-manager, an opportunity to state the obvious.

"We're indoors now," he said, as if a reminder were necessary. "Some of you look as if you're still playing on a full-size pitch outside."

Tanfield Rangers were taking part in the September Sixes, a weekend football festival staged in London. Teams from all over the country had been invited, with Rangers meeting a determined Welsh side, Anglesey Aces, in their opening group game.

The managers wanted all eight members of the squad to sample an early taste of the action and they made two substitutions for the second half.

"You've got to be *spacemen*!" demanded Mr Thomas. "Work hard to make space for each other and the goals will come."

"They'd better do," muttered Ryan. "If I don't score against this lot, I'll shoot myself."

"On this form, you'd probably miss!"

joked Rakesh who had replaced Worm in defence.

"C'mon, team," urged Jacko, the sleeves of his royal-blue shirt tugged up to the elbows. "Plenty of time yet, stay cool."

But the minutes ticked by. The Aces were clinging on to their one-goal lead like a dog with its teeth into a postman's trousers. They wouldn't let go of their grip and Rangers couldn't shake themselves free.

When Speedie, the other substitute, at last put the ball past the giant Aces' keeper, the celebrations were ecstatic. They were also brief. The referee had disallowed the goal.

"Sorry, lads," he said. "The scorer strayed into the area."

The Rangers did well to recover from such a crushing blow. They left it late, but the long-overdue equalizer was worth the wait.

Rakesh began the crucial move, intercepting the ball and playing it forward to Jacko in space. That space was soon closed down.

"Man on!" Rakesh warned.

Jacko shielded the ball with his body and skilfully turned his marker. Glancing up, he saw Ryan and Speedie making good runs off the ball to distract defenders, and the captain decided to go for goal himself. Jacko's sudden burst took the Aces by surprise, but his shot smashed into the boards wide of the target.

The keeper dived in vain and he was still grounded as the rebound was collected by Ryan just outside the area. This time the number nine made no mistake, bulging the unguarded net with the power of his strike.

The Rangers had to settle for a single point from the 1–1 draw.

"Oh well, better than losing, I suppose," sighed Speedie.

"Not much," muttered Dazza, unable to hide his disappointment. "Only the top two teams in each group qualify for the semis, remember."

"And we've got to make sure we're

one of them," said Jacko defiantly. "We want to play as many games as poss this weekend."

"Yeah, that's what we've come here for – loadsa footie!" Ryan insisted. "You hear that, Worm? No getting us mixed up in any of that other stupid business again, right?"

The players stared in the direction of Michael Winter. "I keep telling you, it's got nothing to do with me," Worm complained, pulling a face. "It won't be my fault if anything happens."

They were well aware that something might. It seemed too much of a co-incidence that the eight of them picked for this trip to London were all experienced travellers – *time* travellers...

2 Bookworm

"The College won two–nil," reported Anil, Rangers' left-sided attacker. "And Whizzer scored both the goals."

As soon as their own game was over, Anil had nipped across the sports arena to check on the match between the other two teams in Group A.

The Rangers had met Whizzer before on their travels – and his Victorian ancestor. The modern Whizzer was captain of the squad from a Peak District boarding school where the Rangers had played on their Easter tour.

"Good old Whizzer!" laughed

Rakesh. "He takes some stopping."

"We'll have to try," said Jacko. "We've got the College last and it might well be the decider to see who goes through."

Another four teams were soon battling it out in the opening round-robin games in Group B. The Rangers watched them with interest, picking out some likely dangermen for future reference.

Both the matches ended in draws and the Rangers were raring to get back into action. They began their next game against the white-shirted local team, the Likely Lads, with the same six that finished the Aces game.

"Reckon we'll get on?" asked Anil impatiently. "Hope so."

"All depends," said Worm, fishing out a book from his bag. "Either they need us 'cos they're losing, or they don't need us 'cos they're winning. So which do you want it to be?"

Anil paused to work that out. "Why are you always reading?" he said.

"Why are you always breathing?"

"That's a daft question."

"So's yours. To me, reading's just as vital as breathing."

"Don't you mind people calling you a bookworm?"

"There are worse nicknames than Worm," he said with a shrug.

"I know. I've heard Ryan call you a few of them," Anil giggled and tipped up the book to check the title. It was a history book as usual. *"The Great Fire of London*. Oh, oh! You don't think there's a chance we'll find ourselves in the middle of that, do you?"

"Who knows? This is London. The Fire was in September. Best to be prepared. The more I know about it, the better perhaps..."

Anil shook his head. "Just don't let the others see what you're reading. They'd go berserk. When was this big Fire, anyway?"

"1666. Six hundred years after King Harold lost the Battle of Hastings and three hundred years before England won the World Cup. At least the Fire finished off the Great Plague."

Anil groaned. "Wonderful. That's all I need, getting involved with another plague! Had enough of that kind of thing back at Easter."

As Worm propped himself up against the wall with his book, Anil's attention focused on the football. Rangers had made a good start, keeping possession much better than in the first game and making the Likely Lads do most of the chasing.

"C'mon, Blues," Anil shouted. "Give us a goal."

Speedie almost obliged. He fastened on to a pass from Rakesh and his shot flashed only a fraction the wrong side of a post, scattering the spectators standing beside the goal.

It was their best chance of the half until Jacko scored just before the interval. The goal looked so simple, it made people wonder why most attacks don't result in the ball ending up in the back of the net.

Speedie sprinted down the right and passed inside to Ryan, who let the ball run through his legs to the unmarked captain. 1–0. Easy!

But soccer isn't as free-scoring a game as basketball. Rangers failed to repeat the successful formula, despite adding Anil's dribbling skills to their attack for the last five minutes of the match.

They had to be satisfied with a narrow victory, even though they knew that simply winning wasn't always enough in these tournaments. Qualification often hinged on goal difference or perhaps the number of goals scored.

Leaving Worm still engrossed in his book, they clustered around the results area to study the group table as it was brought up to date.

Group A

	P.	W.	D.	L.	F.	A.	Pts.
College	2	2	0	0	5	1	6
Rangers	2	1	1	0	2	1	4
Aces	2	0	1	1	2	4	1
Likely Lads	2	0	0	2	0	3	0

Whizzer was already there. "We beat the Aces 3–1," he said in greeting. "Nobody can stop us reaching the semifinals now."

"No, but we can still knock you off the top of the table," smiled Stopper, the rock at the heart of Rangers' defence. His dad and Whizzer's had once been schoolmates at the College together and the two lads somehow felt a common bond.

Whizzer laughed. "Wishful thinking, Stopper. If I were you, I'd start saying my prayers that the Aces don't thrash the Lads and catch you up."

"We only need a draw to make us safe."

"Yes, but can you get it against us?" Whizzer said to tease him further. "Your survival might be in our hands!"

Rakesh held out a bar of chocolate. "Are you open to bribes?" he asked with a broad grin.

Rakesh soon found out the answer to that when he was given the thankless job of marking Whizzer. In the very first attack, College's captain scorched past him and hit a shot that Dazza did well to tip over the low crossbar.

"Are you sure you don't want some choc?" Rakesh pleaded as Whizzer trotted back towards him and they both giggled.

Anil and Worm again started as subs,

but Mr Thomas insisted that this time Worm put his book away and watch the game.

"Got a feeling we might need you. I'm not certain Rakesh can cope with Whizzer's trickery."

Worm wasn't confident that he would be able to either. Whizzer looked red hot. The little winger took on Rakesh once more down the boards and whipped over a cross into the middle that neither Jacko nor Stopper could cut out. Rangers were rescued by Dazza's quick reflexes for a second time as the keeper smothered a close-range strike at goal.

Speedie had to spend most of his time in defence, helping Rakesh out, but they still struggled to keep Whizzer quiet. His acceleration made even Speedie seem like a snail with arthritis.

With College so much on top, it came as a shock to everyone, especially Ryan, when Rangers actually took the lead.

Ryan tried to block an intended clearance and turned his back at the last moment as the College defender made contact. The ball struck him full on the bottom and ricocheted past the stranded keeper into the corner of the net.

"*Cheeky* goal, that one!" laughed Jacko as he congratulated the scorer.

Ryan grinned ruefully. "Worth the pain. I don't mind how they go in."

By half-time, however, the scores were level after Whizzer had set up a well-deserved equalizer for his team. And the captain began the second half by shooting the College ahead himself.

Worm was on the pitch to strengthen the defence in a bid to hold out for the precious point, but it was to no avail. Whizzer was simply too good a player to subdue. He bamboozled both Worm and Stopper with his dancing feet and fired the ball home beyond Dazza's dive.

The defenders gaped at one another in

dismay as Jacko collected the ball from the net.

"Forget it," he told them. "But just don't let it happen again, that's all. Our goal difference can't stand the strain."

The College were now content to play out time and save themselves for the knockout stage of the Saturday tournament. They eased up just enough to allow Rangers to enjoy more of the ball – but not enough to let them score another goal.

The losers' hearts sank as the referee blew the final whistle to confirm their 2–1 defeat. The news from the other pitch where the game was still in progress was not good either. The Aces were winning 3–1.

"We've had it now," sighed Dazza. "That's curtains."

3 Knockout

"Don't give up," Jacko urged his team-mates. "C'mon, let's go and cheer on the Lads."

The Likely Lads were not interested in the fate of the Rangers. They were playing purely for their own pride, keen to gain their first point of the afternoon, and they produced a storming finish.

The Aces' manager shouted to his players that the Rangers had lost, but it might have been wiser to keep such information to himself. Now that they knew a place in the semifinals was theirs if the score remained the same, the Aces panicked under the pressure. Instead of continuing to play their normal game, they were kicking the ball anywhere to try and waste time. It proved their undoing.

The Lads were unable to force a draw, but their late consolation goal was worth far more to the watching Rangers. With virtually the last kick of the game, the ball was bundled into the Aces' net and the Rangers celebrated even louder than the supporters of the local side.

"We're through on goal difference!" cried Stopper.

"You beauties!" screamed Jacko. "We owe you one for that, Lads."

The final group tables made happy reading for the Rangers, even if they weren't perhaps as interesting to Worm as *The Great Fire of London*.

Group A

	P.	W.	D.	L.	F.	A.	Pts.
College	3	3	0	0	7	2	9
Rangers	3	1	1	1	3	3	4
Aces	3	1	1	1	5	6	4
Likely Lads	3	0	0	3	2	6	0

Group B

	P.	W.	D.	L.	F.	A.	Pts.
Dynamos	3	2	1	0	6	3	7
United	3	1	2	0	6	2	5
Tigers	3	0	2	1	4	5	2
Double Six	3	0	1	2	3	9	1

"Right, runners-up play the winners of the other group so we're up against the Dynamos in the semifinals," said Mr Stoppard.

"They look a pretty tough bunch from what I've seen of them," added Mr Thomas. "Don't get involved in any rough stuff because you'll come off second best."

"Probably be carried off, by the sound of it!" put in Speedie.

Fortunately for Rangers, it wasn't a close game where tempers might have flared in the tension. Ryan had finally found his shooting boots. It had taken him some time to adjust to the bounce of the ball on the indoor surface, but suddenly everything clicked into place.

Ryan was always hungry for goals, with no thought of passing to a team-mate ever entering his head if he sniffed a scoring chance. And now he was starving. He gobbled the Dynamos up, gorging on the feast of a first-half hat trick.

His appetite still wasn't satisfied, but the happy prospect of helping himself to seconds was snatched away. He was taken off at half-time.

"You've done your job," his dad said by way of explanation when his son complained. "We can't afford to risk you getting crocked before the Final. Some of their tackling has been really wild."

"I was enjoying it," Ryan grinned. "Reckon it was that first dirty foul on me that got my back up. And I sure made them pay for it."

Anil took over the lone striker's role in the second period and was given a bumpy ride. He was pushed, tripped and kicked whenever he had the ball, but from one of the free-kicks Rangers scored again. Jacko tapped the ball to one side and Worm drilled a shot past the unsighted keeper.

The Rangers relaxed their grip on the game after that, enabling Dynamos to grab a goal back that only Dazza was disappointed to concede. He'd wanted another clean sheet. Their 4–1 victory put them in great spirits for the Final, especially when they heard who their opponents would be.

The College had managed to squeeze

past the United team 2–1, but at a cost. Whizzer limped off near the end with a sore ankle.

"I fancy our chances against them now," boasted Ryan as both teams rested for a while. "Revenge will be very sweet!"

The Rangers lined up for the Final in their preferred 2-2-1 formation.

Dazza

Worm   Stopper

Rakesh   Jacko

Ryan

As expected, Whizzer started the game too in the red stripes of the College, but he clearly wasn't fully fit. The ankle injury slowed him up, reducing his threat, although Rangers still gave him plenty of respect. He often found both Rakesh and Worm ganging up on him.

The first half remained goalless, but when Speedie replaced Rakesh after half-time to add extra zip to the attack, the plan backfired.

Whizzer was allowed more room to manoeuvre and Rangers regretted their generosity. Shielding the ball from Worm's challenge, he steered it perfectly into the path of a teammate who was charging forward in support. The boy didn't even have to break his stride as he looked up and hammered the ball past the helpless Dazza.

"He's gone and done us again," groaned Mr Thomas. "That Whizzer is a real star – even on only one leg."

"It's not over yet," said Mr Stoppard. "There's still time."

Rangers needed every minute of it. The referee was already checking his watch as Ryan at last escaped the shackles of his marker.

It was a classic example of the

predator's art. Ryan made space for himself with a dummy run towards goal before suddenly switching direction to meet a cross from Jacko. The finish was instinctive, too, sweeping the ball into the net with a deadly first touch.

"We've got 'em now!" whooped Ryan, hyped up even more than usual after scoring such a goal. "The cup's ours!"

Ryan's claim was somewhat premature. There was extra time to play first and the College boys were equally determined to lay their hands on the Saturday trophy.

Defences held firm and weariness was also a factor at the end of a long afternoon of football. The result was stalemate. The closest either side came to scoring in the extra period was when Dazza had to fling himself across goal to wrap his body around a snapshot from Whizzer.

It was the last save of the game – at least before the drama of the penalty shoot-out!

4   Shoot-out

The Rangers had practised taking penalties in training, but nothing could prepare them for the real thing. This was a nerve-jangling occasion.

Mr Thomas looked at each of the three boys who had been chosen for duty. "Right, it's up to you now. As we agreed, it's Ryan first, then Worm and then Jacko. Good luck."

"I'll need it," Worm muttered under his breath.

"Just do your best. No blame if you miss," Mr Stoppard assured them. "Take some deep breaths and try to relax."

That was easier said than done.

Whizzer looked cool enough, however, as he stepped up to place the ball on the penalty spot. He'd won the toss and decided to have first strike, hoping to lead the way by example. He gave Dazza no chance. His kick fizzed into one corner of the goal as Dazza dived into the other.

Ryan was not to be outdone. He sent the College keeper the wrong way too, punching the air in delight as the ball slapped into the netting.

"One-all," cried the referee, recording the score in a notebook.

All the other players, managers and supporters were lining the pitch, shuffling as close as they were allowed. For those involved, it felt as if the whole world were watching.

A huge roar went up as Dazza blocked the next penalty. He had decided to hold his position this time and fortunately the ball flew straight at him. It was more self-defence than a save.

Now it was Worm's turn to try and be the hero. Running up on jelly-legs, he somehow managed to fool the keeper but scooped the ball wide of the left-hand post. He trailed back to the group, head bowed.

"Never mind," said Mr Stoppard. "Can't be helped. Chin up."

Rakesh wrapped an arm round his shoulders. "Unlucky, Worm," he said. "Dazza and Jacko will repair the damage, you'll see."

Worm could barely bring himself to watch. "Knew I'd be the one to mess things up," he moaned. "I just knew it."

Dazza wasn't even called into action. The College's third kicker blazed the ball over the bar and then sank to his knees in despair. Dazza skipped away towards Jacko and slapped him on the back.

"Finish them off," he grinned. "Keep it low."

As captain, Jacko was the team's usual penalty-taker, although he had to make sure he claimed the ball before Ryan grabbed it. Everything now depended on this kick. If he scored, Rangers had won the cup!

The keeper jumped up and down to ease his tension, but Jacko ignored such distractions. Instead, he focused his mind on where he wanted to put the ball and waited for the whistle.

At the signal, Jacko ran in and made clean contact but saw the keeper fly across his line of fire. The ball clipped the boy's foot, looped up and disappeared over the bar.

Different sections of the crowd groaned and cheered as Jacko stared after the ball in disbelief. He'd never missed a penalty before in his life. He felt numbed.

"Teams are still level," announced the referee. "Sudden death. One penalty each until somebody fails to score."

The dejected captain was inconsolable. "I've let everybody down."

"No, you haven't. It's just one of those things," said Mr Stoppard, trying in vain to raise Jacko's spirits. "They're very small goals. It's not easy to score in them, even from the spot."

The manager glanced across at his son and Stopper could see what was on his mind. He backed away. "Oh, no, don't look at me, Dad. I'm useless at taking pens."

Speedie was brave enough to volunteer, but his courage wasn't rewarded. He gulped as Dazza was well beaten by the first sudden-death penalty, knowing that he now had to score or it was all over.

Under so much pressure, Speedie poked his own effort too near the keeper,

who danced off round the arena with the ball until caught and mobbed by his celebrating teammates. By contrast, Rangers retired quietly to one side of the pitch to lick their wounded pride in private grief.

Whizzer eventually came over to them. "Could have gone either way," he said in consolation. "Better luck tomorrow in the Sunday tournament."

"Thanks," Stopper nodded. "Perhaps we'll meet again then, eh?"

At the presentation ceremony, as the grinning Whizzer held the trophy high to acknowledge the applause, Jacko could only look on in envy.

"That should have been me," he murmured. "If only I'd..."

Mr Thomas cut him short. "No good crying over spilt milk, as they say. We have to pick ourselves up and start all over again tomorrow."

"That's right, we've got to look to the

future now," agreed Mr Stoppard. "What's done is done. It's in the past. You can't change what's already happened."

Worm was listening. "Not so sure about that," he mused. "Nobody knows better than us that time can play some funny tricks..."

"Welcome to the London Planetarium," the recorded voice intoned. *"We hope you will all enjoy your voyage into space..."*

The eight teams attending the Sixes festival were being treated to a special Saturday evening show in the famous Planetarium, the "theatre of the sky". They had just entered the exhibition area and some of the boys were already playing with the video screens and other pieces of equipment on display. The Rangers were not really in the mood.

"What have you brought that for?"

asked Dazza, pointing to the football under Ryan's arm. "Don't think they'd approve of us having a game in here."

"It's his comfort blanket," giggled Rakesh. "Ryan never goes anywhere without a ball."

"Yeah, and he doesn't always come back with it either," said Jacko, referring to the numerous footballs they'd lost on their unscheduled travels on previous tours.

"Well, it's mine, ain't it?" Ryan scowled. "I won it, so I can do what I like with it."

This was true, up to a point, since he'd been awarded the ball as the day's leading scorer with six goals. His dad, however, had other ideas. He'd also laid claim to it as a replacement for one of those that had unaccountably gone missing.

Only Worm was looking forward to the show with any enthusiasm. He'd been to the Planetarium before and knew what to expect. He was also grateful that the trip helped to get his own penalty flop out of his mind.

Over tea at their hostel, he'd tried without success to convince his teammates how good the Planetarium was. "The special effects are amazing. You'd think you really are flying among the stars in a spaceship."

"So what?" Speedie said, unimpressed. "I've seen loads of science-fiction films about space travel. They're all the same."

"This isn't a film. It's sort of virtual reality, all done by computer graphics. It almost feels like you're on a journey through time. . ."

They all groaned. "Oh no, he's off again," sighed Dazza.

Worm wasn't deterred that easily. "Did you know that when you gaze up at the stars, it's like looking back into history? Their light has taken hundreds or thousands of years to reach us!"

"Why's that?" asked Rakesh, grinning. "Missed the last bus, did it, and had to walk all the way here?"

Worm took such sarcastic comments in his stride. He was used to them. "It's because they're so far away," he went on. "And there are billions and billions of stars out there. Space is just so incredibly..."

Worm was searching for the right word to convey such vastness.

"Big?" suggested Anil helpfully.

"*Spacious*, you might even say," Speedie chipped in.

"Plenty of room to kick a ball about by the sound of it," said Ryan.

Worm gave up at last. "Anyway, you'll see for yourselves soon what it's like. You might be in for a few surprises."

That forecast proved to be something of an understatement.

As the footballers began to wander into the main auditorium, they found themselves beneath the enormous copper dome that they'd seen from outside the building. Once everyone was settled into their seats, the Rangers party stretched along the back row, the lights dimmed and the dome came alive.

Anil gasped. "It's full of stars!"

5   Wormholes

The commentary informed the audience what lay ahead.

"We are going to take you on a journey to the stars, travelling through time and space across our Milky Way galaxy and beyond..."

As stars whirled over their heads across the dome at disorientating speed, the viewers were hooked. Even Ryan temporarily forgot about the football that he was nursing on his lap.

"...You will be able to explore the mysteries of a black hole, slipping through a wormhole in the fabric of

space-time to another part of the universe, even to another time..."

"*Wormhole!* Am I hearing things or did he just say the word *wormhole*?" hissed Jacko, his voice carrying along the back row.

"He sure did," Ryan confirmed. "That might explain a lot..."

Despite the darkness of the auditorium, Worm could sense many pairs of inquisitive eyes burning into him. He huddled further down into his seat, wishing the commentary would quickly change the subject.

He had read about wormholes, intrigued by their name, but without really following the scientific theories that supported their existence. Now that the others had heard of them as well, he expected to face some awkward questions later.

At that moment Worm began to feel dizzy and his vision blurred. The sounds

and sights of the star show faded away and he seemed to be floating in the air. A deep black opening had formed in the dome and he was being sucked up towards it like a particle of dust in a vacuum cleaner.

He wasn't alone. He was aware of people around him, his teammates, but they were all swirling along, travelling faster and faster...

As Worm's senses returned with a jolt, he was blinded at first by the harsh lighting and he staggered forwards. Hands steadied him until he regained his balance and he realized who they belonged to.

"Whizzer!" he gasped. "What are you doing here?"

Whizzer was wide-eyed with wonder. "I don't know," he murmured. "I don't even know where *here* is."

Neither did Worm. But he knew it wasn't where they should be.

The eight Time Rangers, plus Whizzer, gazed around the windowless room. The white walls were lined with padded couches, but the only other piece of furniture was a low table, upon which sat a bowl of fruit and a chessboard. None of the boys recognized the strange-looking pieces.

"Brilliant, Worm!" said Ryan sarcastically. "Where have you gone and landed us this time?"

"I don't understand," wailed Whizzer. "What's going on?"

"Good question," muttered Jacko. "Didn't expect to see you here as well."

Stopper sighed. "He was sitting next to me in the Planetarium and he must have got carried away with the rest of us by mistake."

"Join the club, Whizzer," grinned Dazza. "I guess this makes you an honorary member of the Time Rangers."

"Yeah, now you know that the TR on

our soccer kit doesn't just stand for Tanfield Rangers," added Speedie.

Whizzer looked helplessly at Stopper for an explanation, then at Worm.

"Better sit down," Worm said. "This may come as a bit of a shock..."

A section of wall suddenly moved before Worm had a chance to say anything. As far as he was concerned, the interruption was well timed. He didn't have a clue where to start.

A sallow-faced youth appeared in the opening. He was seated in something like a steel-framed armchair, but what caught most of their attention was the fact that it was floating about ten centimetres off the floor. Their mouths gaped in astonishment.

"Welcome to the New Millennium," he stated flatly. He didn't make it sound like much of a welcome.

"Er ... which New Millennium do you mean exactly?" ventured Worm, hardly daring to ask how far into the future they had travelled.

"You have been summoned to the year 3000."

As that brain-curdling information slowly sank in, Stopper garbled several questions that were fighting for air.

"*Summoned?* What do you want from us? Who are you, anyway?"

Ryan backed him up. "Yeah, and why pick on us?"

The youth was selective with his answers. "My students call me Master. Our mind-sensors registered that you have experienced time travel before so the switch was not likely to send you mad. Unfortunately, that has happened to some of our previous *guests*."

The boys were not sure they cared for the way he said that last word. Nor, they suspected, was their state of health of real concern to him.

"How come you're a teacher?" asked

Rakesh. "You can't be any older than us."

"You are correct. I have just twelve Earth summers to my credit, but already I am the Chief Timekeeper. We control our own affairs now."

"*We?*" Rakesh persisted.

"The Chosen Ones," replied Master. "There is nobody on this planet over the age of fourteen."

"What, no adults at all?" gasped Anil. "Where are they?"

Ryan wasn't bothered where they were. "Hey, magic! You mean there's no one around to tell you what to do?"

"Only the Grandmaster of course," he said automatically, but they noticed the first flicker of doubt cross the Master's face.

Before they could fire any more questions at him, he pressed a button on the arm of his hoverchair and the wall began to slide closed.

"Rest," he told them. "You will be needed to perform in one hour."

Master vanished from sight and the footballers were left staring at the bare wall and then at each other.

"Perform? What did he mean by that?" said Anil fearfully.

"Well, I'm not hanging around here for an hour to find out," Ryan blustered. He strode over to the wall but applied the brakes just in time. It refused to open for him, even when he pushed it and gave it a kick.

"Stupid door!" he stormed, slumping on to one of the couches. "Thought it must be one of those automatic jobs."

They all sat down. There seemed nothing else they could do. Nobody felt like having a game of chess.

"Looks like we're trapped," muttered Dazza. "Anyone got any ideas?"

Worm realized they were all looking at him.

"This is all your doing," said Jacko accusingly. "Bet we've come here through one of your wormholes. I knew you were to blame all along."

"How many more times do I have to tell you? I don't know how it keeps happening. I'm not causing it."

"You must be. That's why these things are named after you."

"Pure coincidence," he protested. "Worm's only a nickname."

"Leave off, both of you," Stopper told them. "Arguing won't get us anywhere. What do you reckon's going on, Worm?"

He spread his hands. "Master's the only one who can tell us that. Perhaps we're being used as guinea pigs."

"You mean we could be part of some experiment?"

"Possibly. Maybe they're trying to discover something about us compared to them now. A lot of things must change in a thousand years."

"But how do we get back home?"

The plea came from Whizzer, his thin face ghostly white. They'd almost forgotten that he was still with them.

"Sorry you've got involved in all this business, Whizzer," said Worm, forcing a smile. "If it's any consolation, when this sort of thing's happened before, we've somehow managed to return safely – eventually."

"Huh! There's always a first time," Ryan grunted. "This place gives me the creeps."

The others didn't like to admit they shared the same uncomfortable feeling. They were all silent for a while, pondering their fate, until Rakesh stood up and walked over to the table.

"Fancy an apple?" he asked, offering round the fruit bowl. "An apple for the teacher?"

6 Demonstration

"You bounce that ball again and I'll stuff it down your throat!"

Ryan stopped his repetitive, irritating bouncing, much to everyone's relief. A warning like that from Stopper had to be taken seriously.

If a thousand years had disappeared in the blink of a black hole, the next hour seemed to drag on for ever. When the wall did reopen at last, the boys jumped to their feet as Master drifted into the room on his chair. Following him like a faithful hound was a remote-control trolley.

"You will find everything you need on there," Master said, bringing the trolley to a halt. "My students are waiting for you."

"Waiting for us to do what?" asked Worm. "You still haven't told us why we've been brought here."

"You are going to put on an exhibition."

Worm looked puzzled. "What can *we* possibly show *them*?"

"How to play this game of football of yours," said Master. "It is part of their study course on ancient customs of the past millennium."

"You mean soccer isn't played any more?" grunted Ryan in dismay.

"Ball games died out many centuries ago. Chess is the sport of the people now. A battle of minds, not bodies."

Ryan wasn't listening. He'd removed the lid of one of the cases on the trolley and was holding up a shiny pair of blue shorts and a matching top.

"Well smart," he said. "Wouldn't mind wearing this kit in the Sixes."

"We have had these clothes specially made for you," said Master. "It is time to put them on."

"What if we refuse?" said Jacko defiantly. "What if we don't want to be your performing chimpanzees? You can't make us."

Master's eyes glazed over. He clearly wasn't used to anybody not obeying his commands instantly. He leant his head against a pad on the back of his hover-chair and appeared to be listening.

"Do you wish to return home?" he asked suddenly. His question to Jacko came across more as a threat than an offer.

"Of course we do. And the sooner, the better."

"Then first you must perform."

The footballers were left in no doubt

that negotiations were closed.

"We could report him for kidnapping," Jacko muttered as Ryan tossed him a shirt.

"Just stick that over your head and belt up," snapped Ryan. "You'll only make things worse. What's wrong with having a game of footie?"

"I can't, sorry," said Whizzer. "My ankle's not up to it."

"OK, no problem," Ryan smirked. "You can be ref!"

While they changed, Master was silent, eyes closed and his head resting on the pad. Speedie glanced his way.

"He's dropped off. C'mon, we can leg it."

"Oh, yeah? Where to?" scoffed Dazza. "Do we just dash out into the street and ask where the nearest wormhole station is?"

"I would not advise trying to escape outside," Master said in response. "I was not asleep. Merely receiving further data."

"I didn't hear anything," said Anil.

"Bet it's all in the mind," hissed Speedie. "Y'know, some kind of telepathy."

"Cheaper than using the phone, I suppose," murmured Rakesh.

Stopper drew Worm aside, hoping Master couldn't eavesdrop on their conversation – either physically or mentally.

"I reckon that Grandmaster he mentioned is the guy who's actually pulling the strings here," he whispered. "Master might just be one of his puppets."

"More like one of his pawns, I'd say," replied Worm. "I'm beginning to think this has all got to do with chess some-how."

"How d'yer mean?"

"Well, Grandmaster is the highest

ranking title in chess, right, and—"

Master cut across them. "Time for action," he announced. "Make it a good demonstration and you will be able to leave. Follow me."

"Any chance of a lift in your chair-mobile?" piped up Rakesh cheekily.

There was no reaction. Master swivelled round and set off, showing a surprising turn of speed as he led them along a brightly-lit corridor. They passed a room where the door was open and Worm risked a quick glance inside. Dozens of computer screens were each displaying a game of chess.

"Real bundle of laughs, this Master," said Dazza as they jogged behind him. "I haven't seen his face crack once yet."

"All work and no play makes Jack a dull boy," quoted Stopper.

"Who you calling dull?" Jacko complained.

"I wasn't talking about you. It's just a

saying. If the students are anything like Master, they might well need livening up a bit."

The footballers trotted into the middle of a large hall, its black and white square tiles giving it the appearance of a giant chessboard. The sound of their trainers on the patterned floor echoed in the silence, but the hall wasn't empty. It was lined with children, aged between about seven and ten, sitting straight-backed in rows of their own chairs.

"They obviously haven't got Master's de luxe model," chuckled Speedie. "They're not hovering."

"Probably just parked," said Dazza. "Bet nobody walks in this place."

The young boys and girls stared in amazement at the oddly-dressed strangers who stared straight back at them.

"They're like robots," muttered Jacko. "They might at least have applauded our entrance."

Ryan suddenly smashed his football high up into the air against the ceiling, cracking one of the light fittings.

"Hey, you kids!" he yelled at the top of his voice. "Wake up! It's time for a change round here. You ain't never seen nothing like this..."

Ryan was quite right. The students had been taught about the rules of football, as far as their teachers understood the game from surviving records. There was even a set of small, netted goals at each end of the hall. But what they soon saw happening in front of their own goggling eyes took them by complete surprise. It stunned the watching teachers, too.

The players began to charge about the hall, kicking and heading a bouncing sphere. And they were shouting and laughing at each other as they ran. It all looked like ... well, fun. Even though the baffled spectators were not quite sure of the meaning of the word.

"GOOOAAALLL!" screamed Ryan each time he scored, jumping up and punching the air in an even more exaggerated fashion than usual.

The Rangers were enjoying themselves, despite the bizarre situation. They'd quickly organized a four-a-side game to parade their skills, half of them pulling off their tops to play as "skins". They were determined to show the chairbound, soccer-starved audience what they were missing.

Jacko launched another attack by clipping the ball out wide to Anil who shot before Stopper could make a challenge. Worm was in goal for Stopper's side and dived full-length to his left to cling on to the ball.

He hurled it forwards for Ryan to chase and the striker stormed past Rakesh, cut inside and then lashed the ball at goal. Dazza parried the shot but, as he scrambled for the rebound, Ryan's knee accidentally caught the keeper in the face.

Dazza lay flat out, an impressive amount of blood pouring from his nose and one eye already beginning to swell.

"Soz, Dazza, didn't mean to," Ryan tried to apologize, helping him to sit up.

"Show him the red card, ref," Anil appealed to Whizzer. "Send him off!"

For the first time, the players noticed a buzz among the students.

"Got the crowd going at least," said Rakesh. "Maybe they've never seen real red blood before!"

Master cruised towards them. "Continue the exhibition," he ordered, signalling two of the older students, a boy and a girl, to approach. "He will be taken to be repaired."

"Repaired? He's not a machine, you know," said Stopper. "He just needs some water, cotton wool and a bit of TLC."

"TLC?"

"Yeah, that's tender loving care," Speedie translated as Dazza hitched a ride on one of the hoverchairs as they began to glide away.

"Think I'll go with him and see if they can fix my ankle," said Whizzer. "I want to be fit for tomorrow's tournament."

"No rush," Jacko told him. "Tomorrow's a thousand years ago."

7 Space

"Who's in goal now?" said Anil.

"One of the robots," laughed Rakesh. "It's about time they did something instead of just sitting there."

"Hey!" Jacko shouted out. "Anybody want to play?"

It seemed to be an offer that they *could* refuse. But then, slowly and timidly, a number of the students raised their hands.

"Great. We'll have all five of you. Come on down," Jacko urged before Master or any of the teachers could make a move to stop them.

The volunteers hovered towards the pitch and one of them pointed shyly to the goal. She gave the players a nervous smile.

"So you *are* human after all," grinned Rakesh. "Do you speak as well?"

The girl nodded.

"Right, prove it. What's your name?"

"Leela."

"OK, Leela, can you catch a ball?"

"I do not know."

"Well, I guess we'll soon find out," he said and gave her chair a little kick. "But first you'll have to get out of that thing."

Leela looked alarmed. "We're not allowed to."

"Yes, you are to play football. Hoverchairs aren't in the rules."

She hesitated and Rakesh recalled seeing a life-size model at the Planetarium of the first man to set foot on the Moon. As a joke he twisted Neil Armstrong's famous words.

"You can do it," he encouraged her. "One small step for a girl, one giant leap for humankind!"

Leela giggled, then stood up and stepped away from the chair. The others followed her daring example and the footballers moved the chairs away before the children could change their minds.

The students were shared between the teams and the game continued almost at walking pace. The new recruits were not used to any physical activity, but they did their best to join in and kick the ball when it came near them. The Rangers heaped praise on any successful contact with the ball, even if it didn't go in the right direction.

"Well saved!" Rakesh called out when Leela managed to gather up a weak lob from Speedie. "You'll make a good goalkeeper."

She smiled across at her friends in the audience and plucked up the courage to

wave at them. To her amazement, they waved back.

Master watched the performance with fascination. He had never seen the students so excited. More of them wanted to take part and chairs were now swiftly abandoned. Even some of the teachers joined in as well. The kickabout became a noisy free-for-all, with hands in use as much as feet. Rules no longer mattered.

"Looks like we've just reinvented the

game of football," Worm chuckled. "This is the way it began yonks ago in those medieval rough and tumbles."

The Time Rangers knew all about them. They'd already played in one.

Soon there were far too many people on the pitch to make it safe to continue. Just as Jacko went over to speak to Master, the ball burst.

"If you've got any spare balls, we could play outside where there's more space," he suggested.

Master's face creased into an attempt at a smile. "More space, yes, but it is not possible, I am afraid," he said, without giving a reason. "We have made some footballs, however, for you to use in here."

The Rangers began an impromptu coaching session. Each of them took a group of students to practise certain skills and the youngsters shrieked with laughter at their own mistakes. Dazza and Whizzer could scarcely believe their eyes, or their ears, when they returned to the hall.

"What's come over this lot?" gasped Dazza.

"Looks like your teammates have managed to stir things up a bit," laughed Whizzer. He felt much happier now that his ankle had received a spell of heat treatment that seemed to have worked a miracle cure.

Stopper greeted them, breaking off from supervising heading practice. "I think we've just caused a revolution," he grinned. "Either that, or we've just set back the course of civilization a few hundred years."

Ryan left his group having shooting practice, including goalscoring celebrations, to check on his victim. "How's the face?" he asked, peering at Dazza's swollen eye. "They've not made you any prettier."

Dazza yelped as Ryan reached out to examine the eye. "Don't touch it. You've already done enough damage. They dealt with my cut lip and nosebleed, but can't do much about all the bruising."

"Wonder how we're gonna explain that to my dad," Ryan grunted.

"Not sure whether we'll ever get a chance to," said Dazza ominously. "I sat in one of those hoverchairs while I was having some first aid and didn't like it one bit."

"Why? What happened?" asked Stopper.

"I rested my head against that pad at the back, right, and it felt dead weird. Almost as if something was exploring my brain."

"Don't suppose it found much," grinned Ryan.

"This isn't funny," Dazza insisted. "I'm serious. I think it was trying to take over my mind."

"Good job I was there," said Whizzer. "I saw he was struggling to get out of the chair so I pulled him up. He'd gone all pale."

"Bet it was the Grandmaster," said Stopper. "He must be controlling all these kids the same way. Y'know, sort of brainwashing them!"

"Yeah, and the longer we stay here, the more chance he'll have to try and get us under his thumb, too," Ryan snarled.

Master called a halt to the session at that moment. Many of the students were flagging or flopping back into their chairs through exhaustion and overexcitement. Their unfit bodies needed to rest.

As the students left the hall, Dazza told the other Rangers about his experience. They were now all on their guard.

"Thank you, that was most ... interesting," Master said. "We would like you to stay with us for a while to help us practise these ball skills."

Stopper protested immediately. "You promised we could go once we'd done the demonstration. Now keep your side of the bargain."

"Yeah, we know what your game is here," said Worm. "And I'm not talking about football either. We've got you in check!"

Master gave a strange, lopsided smile. It was clearly something else he would have to practise. "But not checkmate," he replied, making an effort at a joke. "I still have a choice of moves. Come with me, *please*."

They hadn't heard him use that important word before, but they remained suspicious of his motives.

"We want to get back to our own time," Jacko demanded. "Where on earth are you taking us now?"

"Nowhere. You are not on Earth at all!"

8 Changes

"Would you like to use chairs?" asked Master, trying to appear friendly.

"No way," answered Whizzer. "We'll walk to wherever we're going."

"Good idea. I think I will, too."

Master got to his feet rather shakily and led the boys slowly across the hall. That was all the walking they had to do. The rest of the journey was by lift, escalator and a sliding corridor like a conveyor belt.

"We have reached the main observation tower at the top of the building," Master told them, opening a door.

"Enjoy the view."

It was the first time they had been able to look out of a window since their arrival. This window certainly made up for it. It was huge, stretching all around the circular dome.

The travellers gazed out of it in bewilderment at the barren, rocky landscape. Reddish boulders littered the surface as far as the mountains on the distant horizon.

"This is what you used to call the Red Planet," said Master. "Mars."

"You ... you mean – you're Martians?" stammered Anil.

Master laughed out loud. "No, we are all Earthlings, just like you. Mars is now the ABC – the Advanced Base for Chess. The Chosen Ones come here at seven years of age for specialist training, away from all family distractions and the temptations of life on Earth."

"You mean all you do here is play

chess?" said Worm.

"Chess and study. To teach and to learn. These are our peak years. Star chess players must make many personal sacrifices and have great self-discipline to excel at the sport."

"And to be able to think for themselves," added Stopper pointedly.

Master sighed. "Now I am away from my chair, I can speak more freely. I fear we may have gone too far. It seems that we have forgotten an old saying of yours – a healthy body means a healthy mind."

"Do you always have to obey the Grandmaster?" asked Jacko.

"No, but he has made Earth into one of the best chess-playing worlds in the whole Galaxy. Now he wants us to be the very best. The ABC is his way of achieving that goal."

"I reckon soccer goals are better ones to have," put in Ryan.

Master surprised them by agreeing.

"After what I saw today, I believe you may be right. Things must change here. We need to have more fun in our lives. Perhaps it will even help us to become better at chess, too."

"Incredible!" breathed Ryan as the view from the window became obscured by a swirling storm of red dust. "Just think – we're the first people ever to play footie on Mars!"

"That's what you really call an away match!" laughed Anil.

"And thanks to you," said Master, "I am sure that we will take the game back to Earth. Football might well spread all over the Milky Way now."

"Soccer stars of the future!" grinned Rakesh.

Worm conjured up an image of the students and teachers reintroducing the game to the people on Earth. He couldn't resist a smile.

"Football's coming home!"

So were the Time Rangers – and Whizzer!

Master, in his role as Chief Time-keeper, arranged for a wormhole to be specially created to convey the footballers back through the centuries. They only just had time to finish changing into their own clothes.

"Shame we can't take this kit home with us," said Dazza.

"I've already got my souvenir," chuckled Rakesh, showing his pal a present from Leela. He slipped it into his coat pocket as Master floated into the room.

Worm was busy examining the chessboard on the table, sorely tempted to help himself to one of the oddly-shaped pieces. He guessed now that they represented alien life-forms from other star systems. He stepped away guiltily, hoping Master wasn't able to read his mind, and was relieved to see that the head pad had been removed from the chair.

Master gave a little nervous cough before speaking. "Um, I think I ought to inform you that you may not find things quite how you left them."

"Oh, great!" muttered Jacko. "You can't guarantee just where – or when – we might end up?"

"I did not say that. You will be returned to the Planetarium at the exact nanosecond that you departed. Other people will not even have been aware of your disappearance, it happened so quickly."

"So what's the problem?" asked Worm.

"Wormholes are warps in spacetime," Master explained. "You go in one end of the tunnel and pop out the other – but you may emerge in a slightly different ... um ... world. Nothing alarming, I promise. In fact, you may not even notice the changes."

"Changes?" Worm repeated the word anxiously.

"We exist in a multiverse, not a universe. Other worlds reflect how things might have been if you had followed a different course of action at some point in time."

"You mean, sort of parallel universes? That's science-fiction stuff."

Master shook his head. "Science fact now."

Ryan gave up trying to understand what they were talking about. He gazed sadly at his punctured football. "Well, I hope this is different when we get back or Dad's gonna be dead mad."

Master smiled. He was beginning to get better at it. "You might be, too. You may well have no memory of this trip."

"What! Are you telling us we'll forget all that's happened here?" gasped Stopper. "That's ridiculous!"

"It is for your own good. It might be too confusing otherwise if some changes have occurred."

"I'm confused already," admitted Anil. "C'mon, let's just get back."

Master bowed his head. "As you wish," he said, pressing a button on the chair control panel. "*Bon voyage*, Time Rangers. I'm sure football will become as big as chess in the New Millennium..."

They didn't have a chance to reply. A gaping black hole opened up in the ceiling and they felt the same disorientating sensations as before. The next thing they knew, they were sitting in the back row of the Planetarium.

"*We might think of a wormhole tunnel as a kind of short cut through space and time,*" continued the commentary. "*But of course we all know that time travel, as such, is not really possible...*"

The Rangers glanced at each other and

sniggered. Rakesh caught sight of Dazza's face. "You've got a shiner," he said. "A great big black eye."

"What! You're kidding."

"No, straight up."

Dazza put a finger up to his right eye and flinched. "Ow! Dunno how that's happened."

"Sshhh!" whispered Mr Thomas. "Shut up, you two. Watch the show and you might learn something."

It was only when the presentation ended and the lights came back on that Ryan let out a wail of complaint. "Hey! This ball's gone flat. What a swizz! They must've given me a duff one."

"You're a jinx when it comes to footballs," grumbled his dad. "They don't seem to last five minutes when you get hold of them."

"Magic show!" enthused Anil as they stood on the pavement outside, waiting to be taken back to the hostel. "That roller-coaster ride through the black hole was fantastic."

"It seemed so real," said Whizzer, shaking his head in wonder. "I feel like I've actually been on some incredible adventure."

"Yeah, I know what you mean," said Speedie. "I'm knackered."

His yawn set the others off. "Need to get some kip and be fresh for tomorrow's tournament," said Stopper. "How's the ankle, Whizzer?"

"Fine now. Sitting down in there for a while must have done it good. Anybody fancy a game of chess at the hostel?"

"Sure," said Dazza. "Don't normally like to play chess, but I'm just in the mood for a game for some reason."

"You ought to get some beauty sleep with that eye of yours," Rakesh giggled. "About a month of it!"

He suddenly produced an object from his pocket and stared at it in puzzlement.

"What have you got there?" Worm asked him, showing interest. "Did you buy it in the souvenir shop?"

"Bet he nicked it!" cut in Dazza to get his own back for the taunt.

"No, I didn't. What would I want with a lump of old rock?"

"Looks like one of those rock samples from the Moon – or even Mars," said Worm seriously. "I've seen pictures of them in space books."

"Don't be stupid. I've just fished it out of my coat. No idea how it got there." Rakesh gave the rock to Worm. "You can have it if you want."

Worm studied the piece of red rock closely. As he turned it over and over in his hands, it seemed to trigger off vague memories. There was a nagging thought in the back of his mind that something wasn't quite right, but the arrival of the coach caused him to shrug it off.

As expected, he had to put up with some ribbing on the journey about wormholes. "Might even decide to become a space scientist," he announced.

"Thought you were going to be a historian," said Speedie.

"I am. But if these wormholes do exist, I might be able to keep nipping back in time and studying some period of history at firsthand."

"It's amazing!" said Ryan. "We've been away nearly a whole day and he hasn't dragged us off on any more of his time-travelling jaunts yet."

"Give him time ... er ... so to speak," laughed Stopper. "He'll find some excuse to disappear. We'd better just tell the driver not to hit any wormholes in the road!"

As Worm walked into the hostel dormitory, his eye was caught by the silver trophy on the captain's top bunk. He did a double take as if he couldn't quite believe what he was seeing.

Jacko grabbed the cup and held it above his head. "What a start to the weekend!" he cried. "Couldn't have worked out better today."

"OK, OK, just 'cos you scored that winning penalty in the shoot-out," grinned Anil. "We were there too, remember. We saw how close the goalie was to saving it, so there's nothing to boast about."

"Yeah, bet you'd have kept well quiet if you'd gone and missed like Worm," cackled Ryan. "You'd be as sick as a parrot if it'd cost us the cup. Can you imagine?"

Jacko gave a shudder. "Ugh! Thought I did then just for a second. Dead weird feeling, you know what I mean?"

Worm nodded, turning pale. "Yeah, I think I do."

Jacko glanced at him and then back at the cup. He shook his head as if trying to clear it. "Something's happened, hasn't it?" he said softly. "Feels different, somehow."

Ryan broke the spell. He booted his misshapen ball in disgust into the corner of the room. "Pity about that!" he cried, scrambling up to his top bunk and stretching out. "Still, it's been a wicked day. Going to the Planetarium was a great idea after all."

"Why's that?" asked Anil, half-guessing what was coming.

"'Cos the Rangers are over the Moon!"

TIME RANGERS

Follow our Time Rangers into the past with book
8. A Fate Worse Than Death.

Jacko was racing along a rutted track, taking a short cut he knew would bring him out near the orchard. The blood was pounding in his ears, but he could hear a droning noise in the sky, a noise that was getting nearer and nearer. And there she was.

Alice was leaving the orchard with a basketful of apples and picking her way around the edge of the potato crop. The droning was now even louder and he saw her shield her eyes from the sun to look up.

"It's a German bomber!" he yelled. "Get down!"

She laughed. "Don't be silly. We don't have Germans on our farm."

Jacko was gasping for breath as he stumbled across the field furrows. Alice could see the panic in his eyes as he approached and she screamed. Jacko reached her at full speed, almost knocking her over, but he managed to grab her with both arms. He lifted her up off her feet and kept on running, sending the apples and the football flying into the air.

"Oh, God, I've left it too late," he cried, finding Alice heavier than he expected. "I'm not gonna make it in time..."